LYDIA MARIA CHILD

Over the River and Through the Wood

ILLUSTRATED BY DAVID CATROW

HENRY HOLT AND COMPANY • **NEW YORK**

Henry Holt and Company, LLC / Publishers since 1866
115 West 18th Street / New York, New York 10011
Henry Holt is a registered trademark of Henry Holt and Company, LLC
Illustrations copyright © 1996 by David Catrow. All rights reserved.
Published in Canada by Fitzhenry & Whiteside Ltd.,
195 Allstate Parkway, Markham, Ontario L3R 4T8.
Library of Congress Cataloging-in-Publication Data
Child, Lydia Maria Francis, 1802–1880 [Boy's Thanksgiving Day]
Over the river and through the wood / by Lydia Maria Child; illustrated by
David Catrow. Summary: An illustrated version of the poem that became
a well-known song about a journey through the snow to grandfather's
house for Thanksgiving dinner. 1. Thanksgiving Day—Juvenile poetry.
2. Children's poetry—American. 3. Children's songs—Texts.
[1. Thanksgiving Day—Poetry. 2. American poetry. 3. Songs.]
I. Catrow, David, ill. II. Title. PS1293.B68 1996 811′.3—dc20 96-2102
ISBN 0-8050-6311-0 / First Owlet paperback edition—1999
First hardcover edition published in 1996 by Henry Holt and Company
Printed in the United States of America on acid-free paper. ∞

1 3 5 7 9 10 8 6 4 2

To Kirby,
my best friend
—D. C.

Over the river and through
the wood,
To grandfather's house we go;

The horse knows the way
To carry the sleigh
Through the white and drifted snow.

Over the river and through the wood—
Oh, how the wind does blow!
It stings the toes
And bites the nose,

As over the ground we go.

Over the river and through the wood,
To have a first-rate play.

Hear the bells ring,
"Ting-a-ling-ding!"

Hurrah for Thanksgiving Day!

Over the river and through the wood
Trot fast, my dapple-gray!

Spring over the ground,
Like a hunting hound!
For this is Thanksgiving Day.

Over the river and through the wood,
And straight through the barnyard gate

We seem to go
Extremely slow—
It is so hard to wait!

Over the river and through the wood—
Now grandmother's cap I spy!

Hurrah for the fun!

Is the pudding done?

Hurrah for the pumpkin pie!